# ·Tough Ma[ze]

Have fun as you wind your way through each intricate maze.
Don't be fooled by mazes with multiple points; there's
only one way out! Solutions at the back of the book.

Copyright © 1989 by Scott Sullivan.
Published by Troubador Press, a subsidiary of Price Stern Sloan, Inc. Los Angeles, California.

ISBN: 0-8431-2332-X

10 9 8 7 6 5 4 3

## by Scott Sullivan

**TROUBADOR PRESS**
*a subsidiary of*
PRICE STERN SLOAN

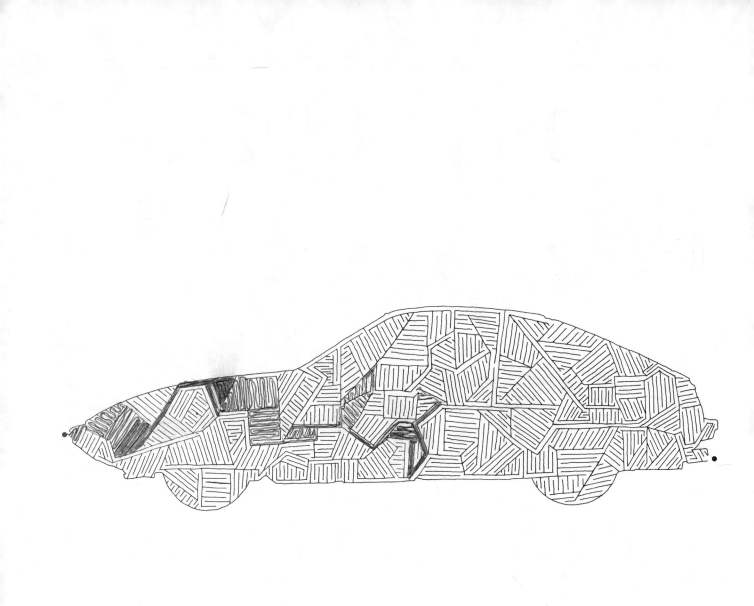

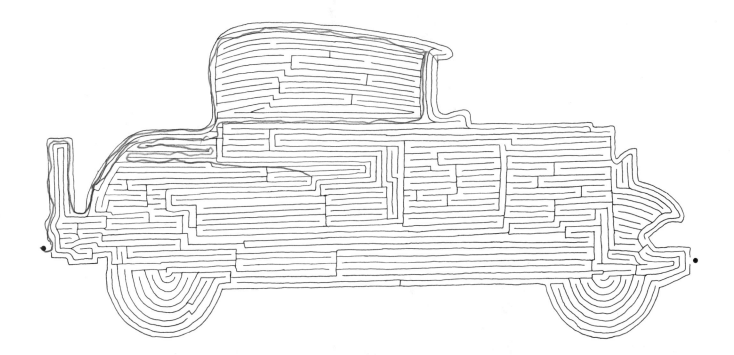

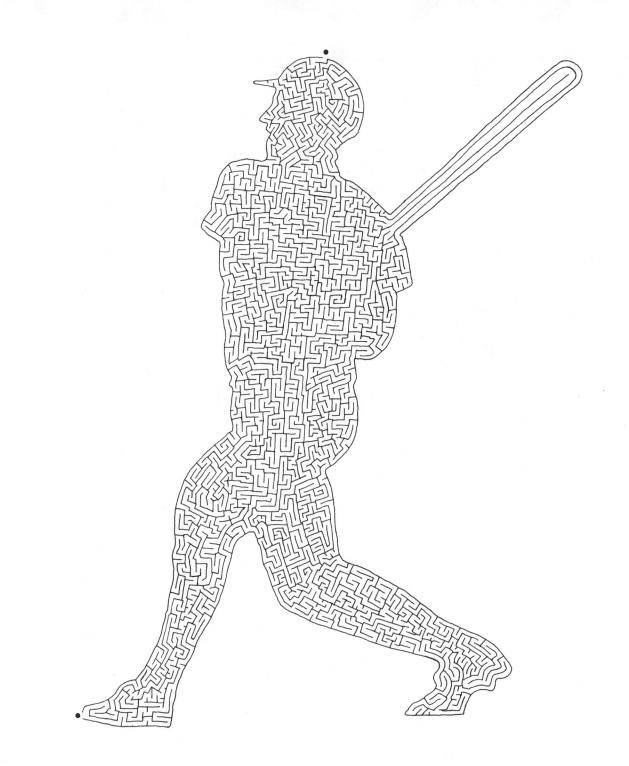

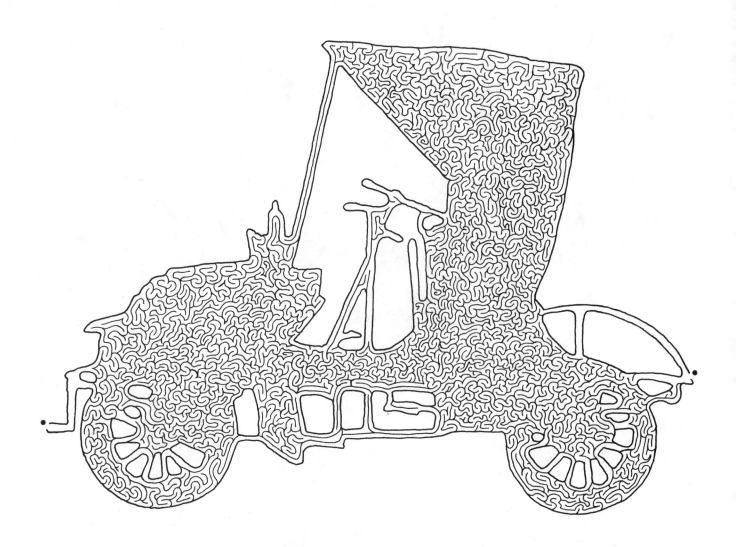

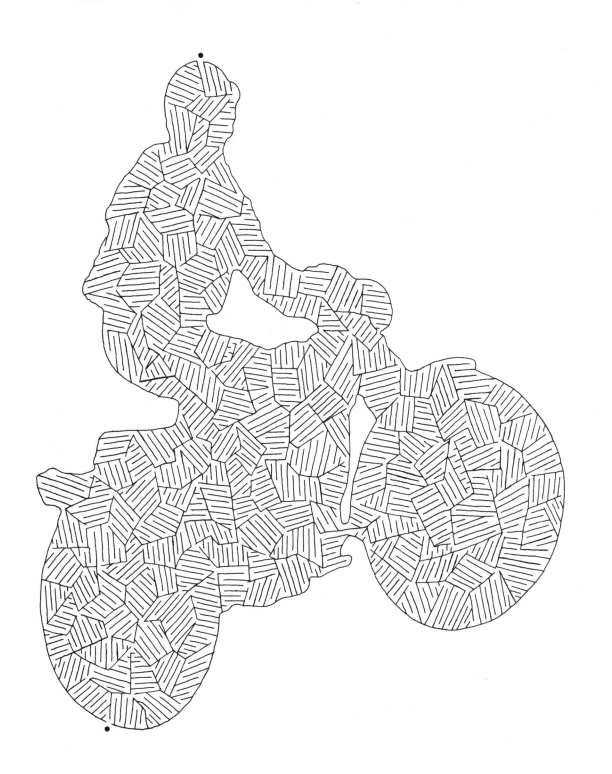

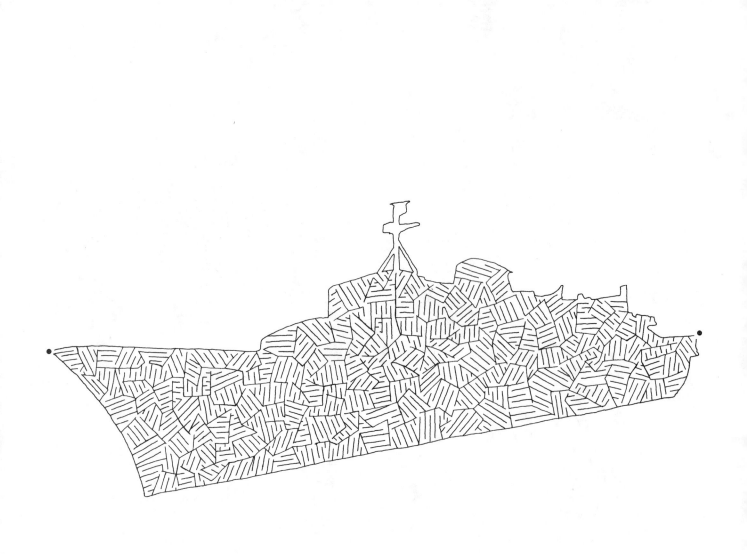

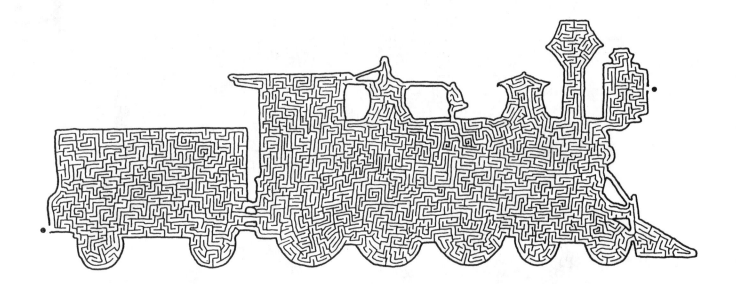

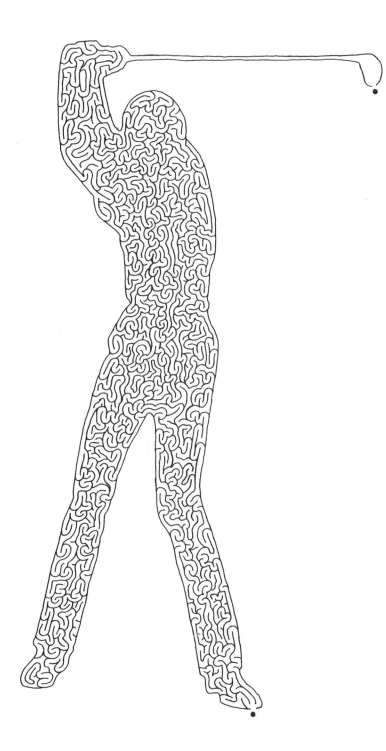

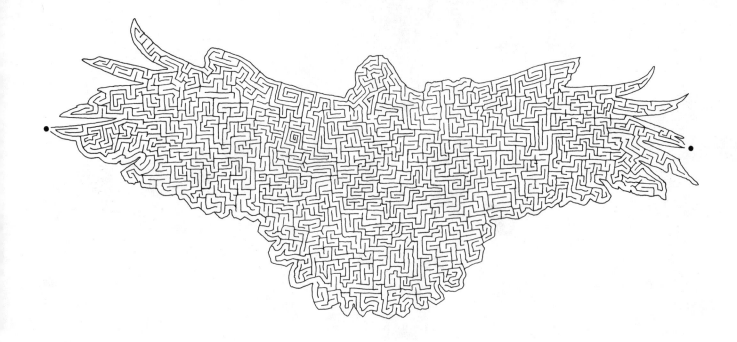

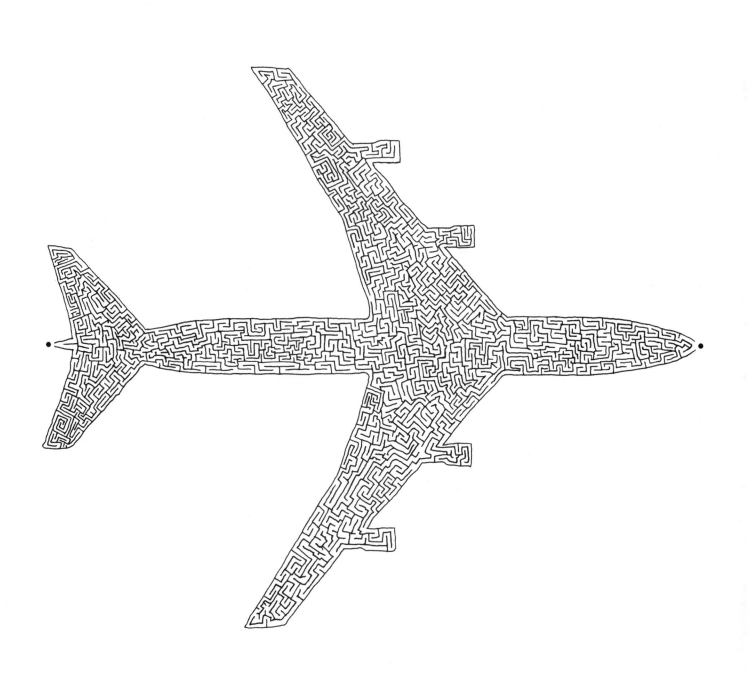

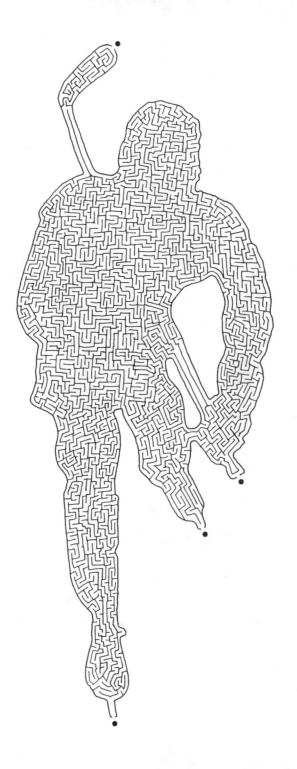

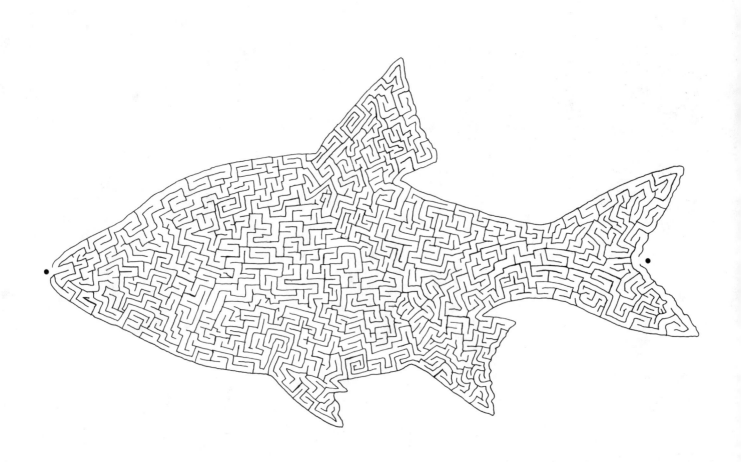

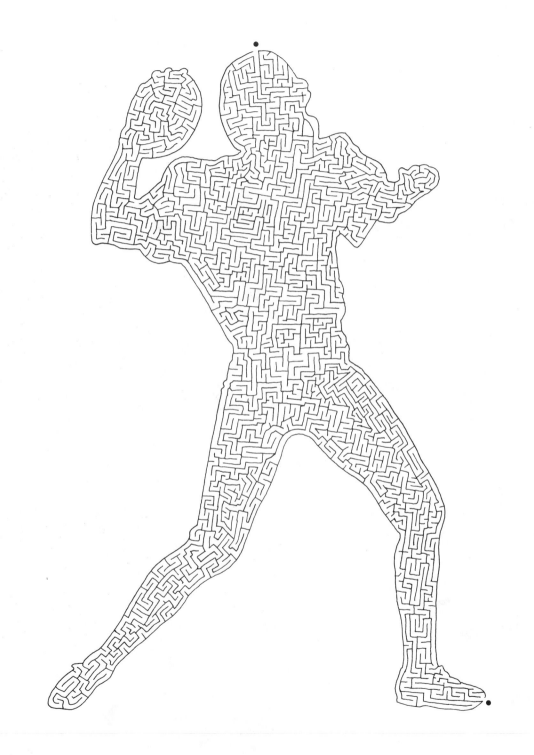

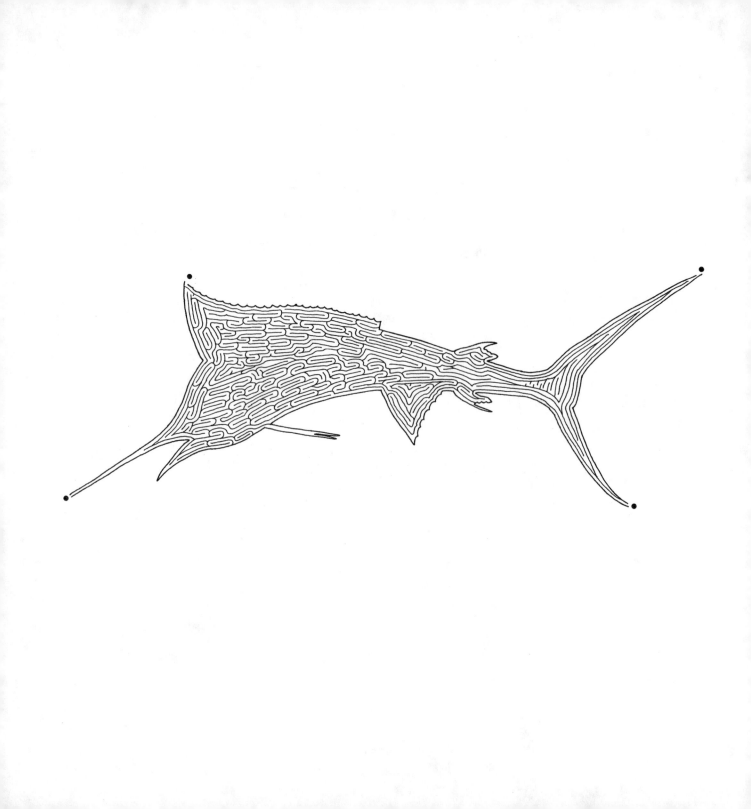

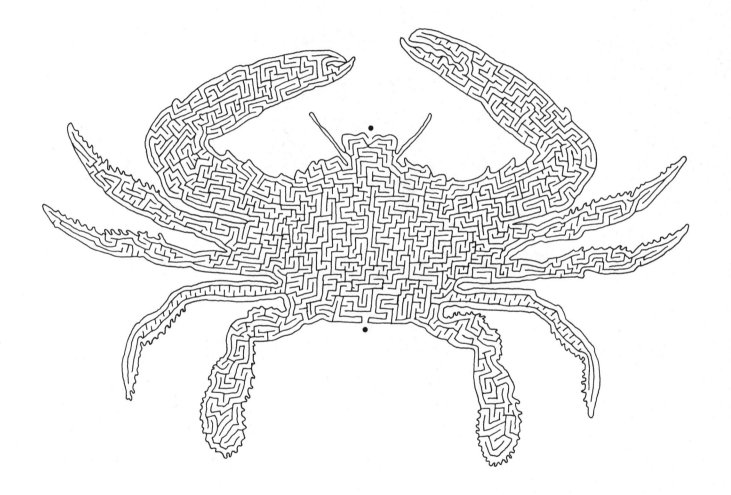

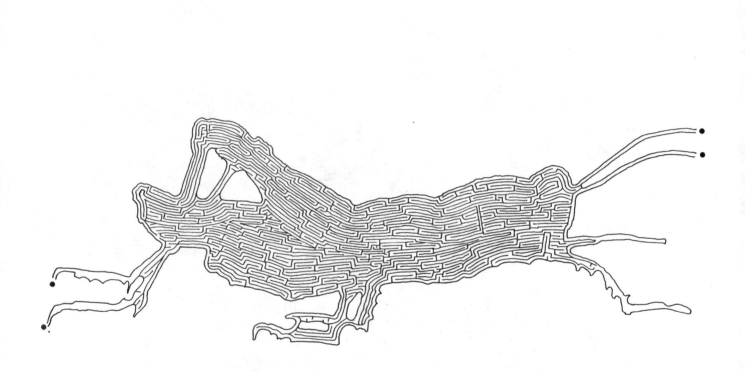

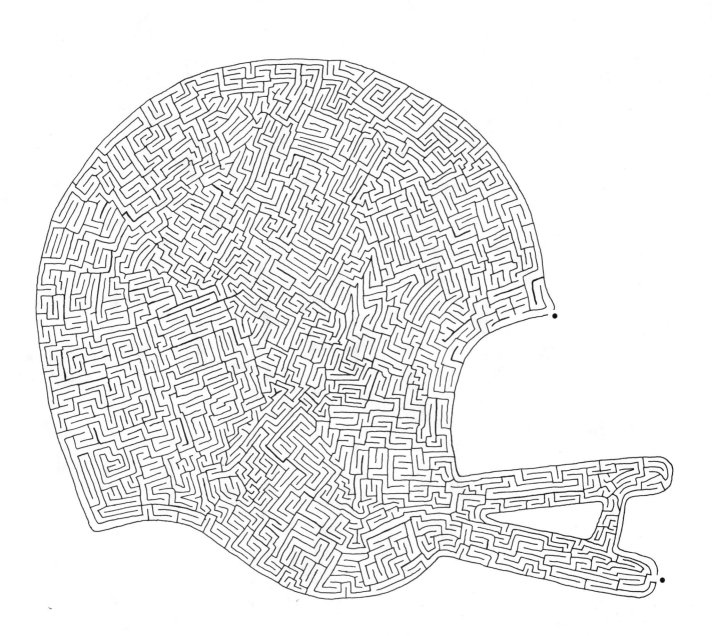

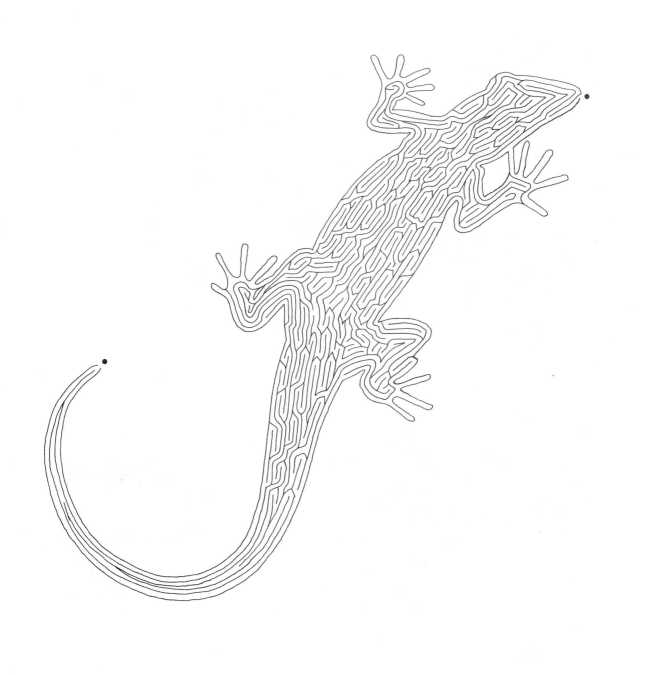

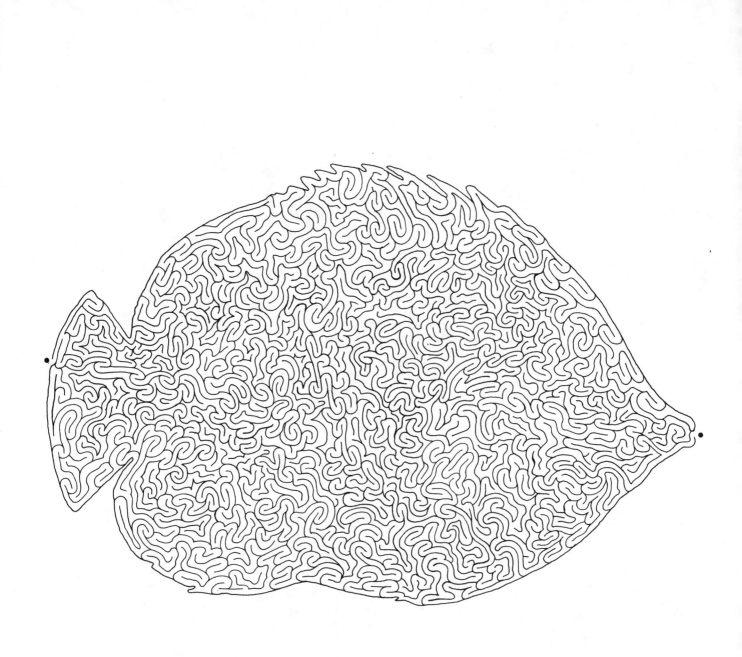

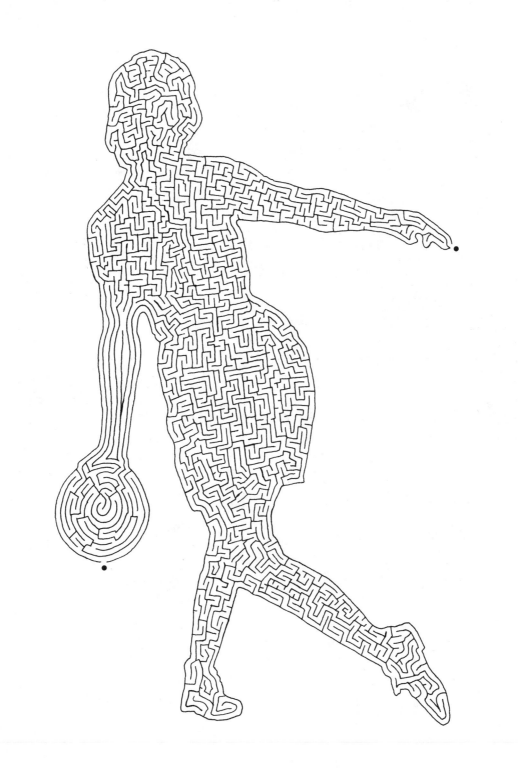

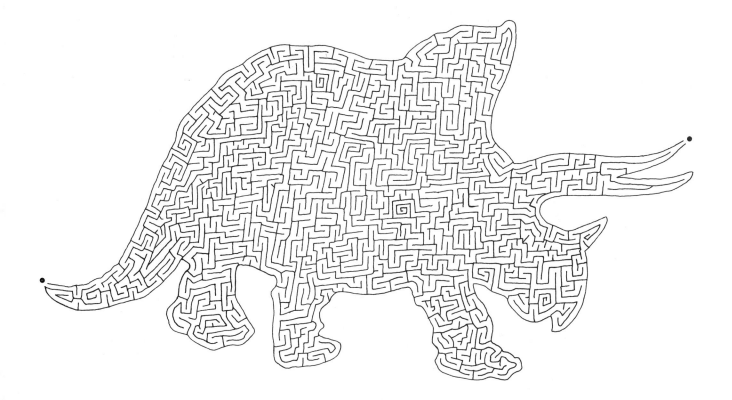

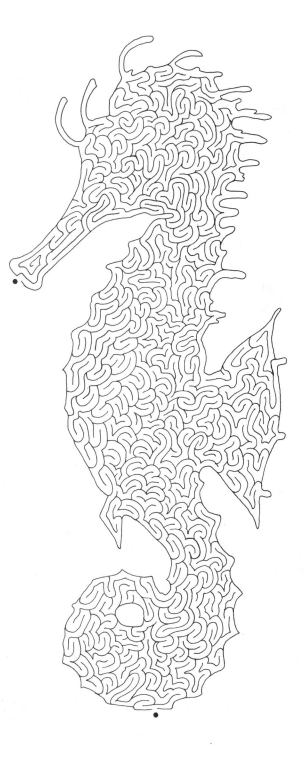

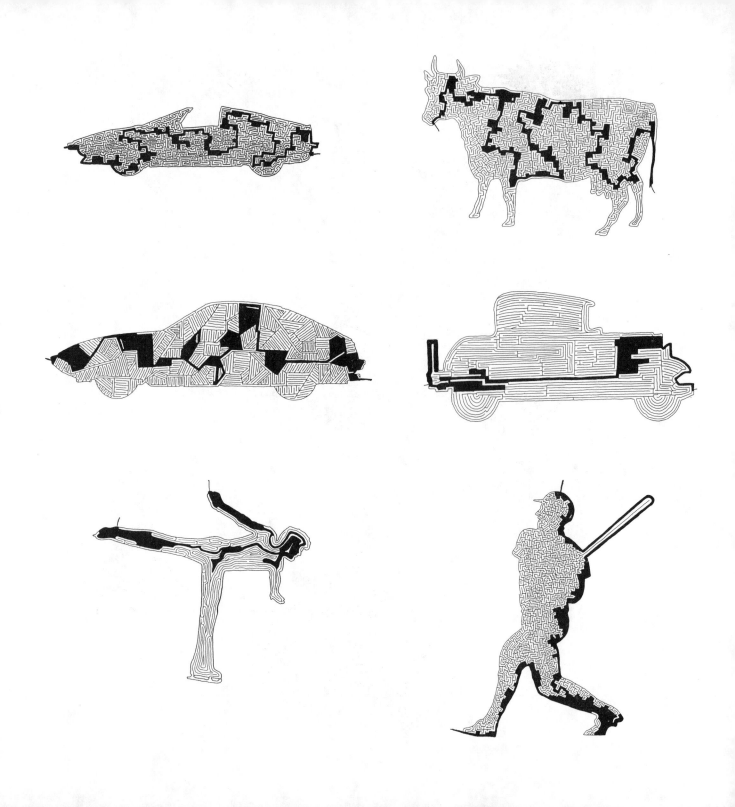

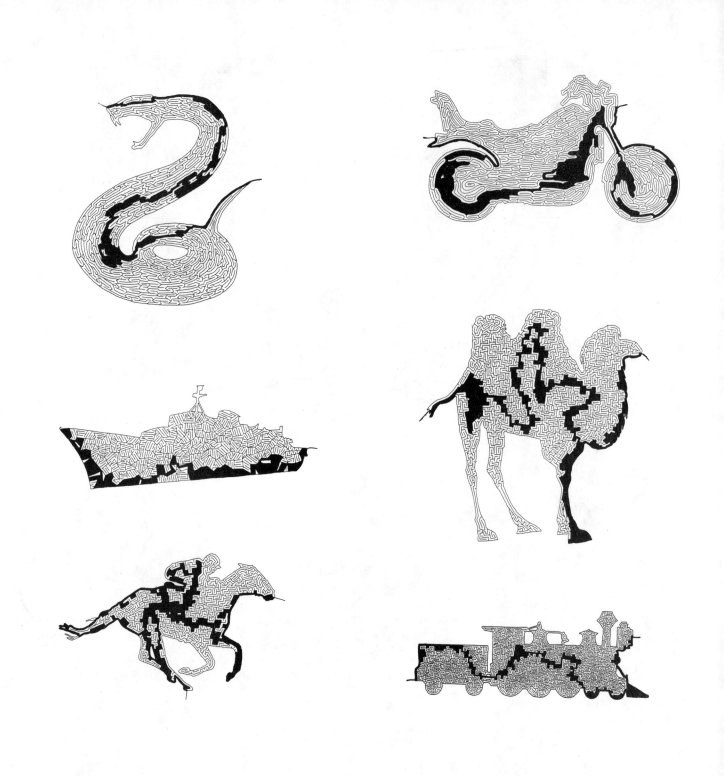

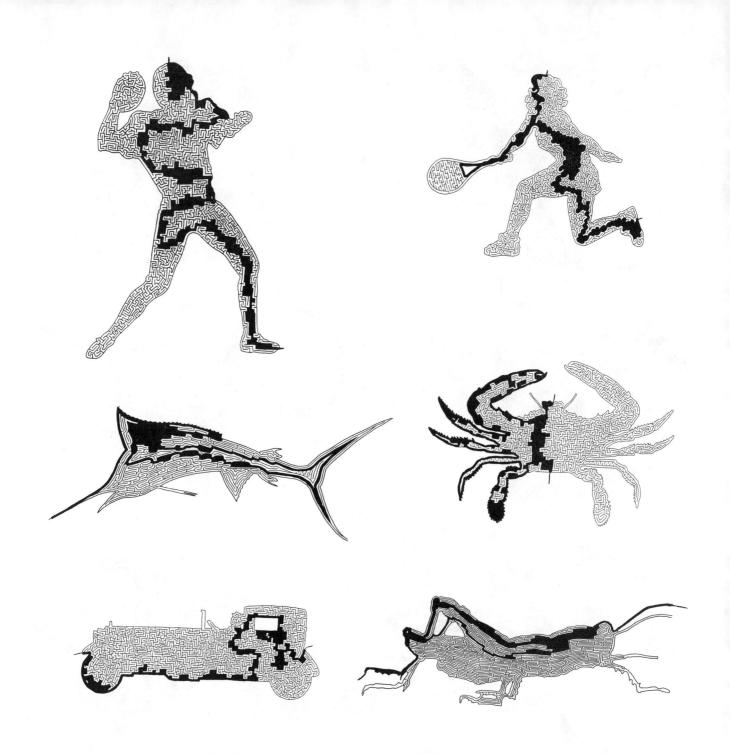

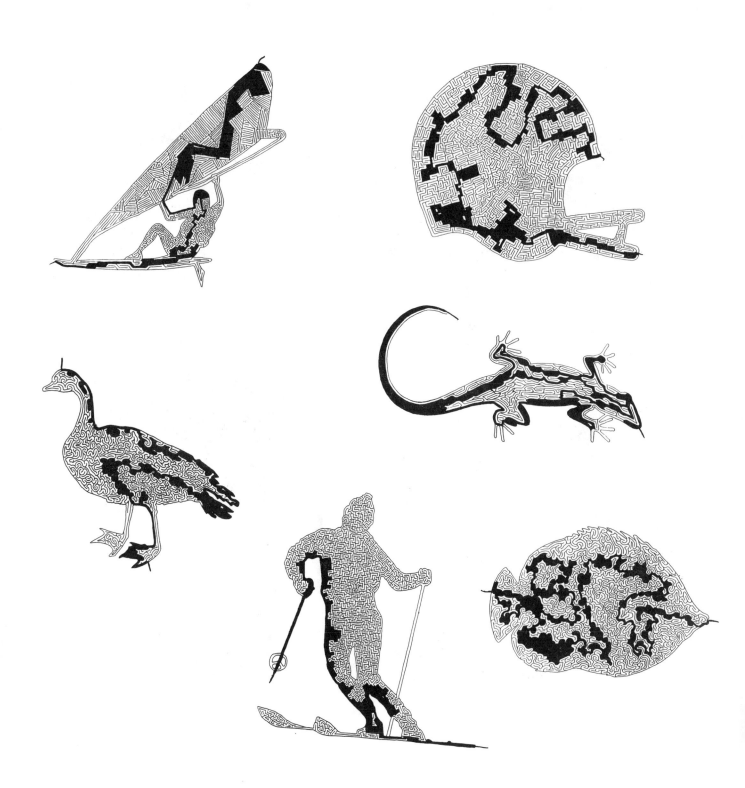